The Dream Machine

Written by
Jenny Jinks

Illustrated by
Lilia Miceli

Chapter 1

Ava pulled her duvet over her head to hide the light from her torch. She listened to her mum's footsteps getting closer. It was well past Ava's bedtime, and she would be in serious trouble if her mum knew that she was still awake this late. Especially when she had school the next day.

The Dream Machine

'The Dream Machine'
An original concept by Jenny Jinks
© Jenny Jinks

Illustrated by Lilia Miceli

Published by MAVERICK ARTS PUBLISHING LTD
Studio 11, City Business Centre, 6 Brighton Road,
Horsham, West Sussex, RH13 5BB
© Maverick Arts Publishing Limited February 2021
+44 (0)1403 256941

A CIP catalogue record for this book is available at the British Library.

ISBN 978-1-84886-786-4

www.maverickbooks.co.uk

This book is rated as: Grey Band (Guided Reading)

But Ava could never resist reading just one more chapter of her book... or maybe two.

Ava held her breath as the footsteps paused for a moment outside her door. She pushed the torch further under the covers to be safe. It rolled away down the bed and out of sight. Ava stayed as still as possible until she heard her mum's footsteps move away, and her bedroom door close. She felt around under the duvet to find her torch. But it must have rolled further than she thought. She dived further down the bed, chasing the light as it rolled further and further away. Ava was sure she should have fallen off the end of the bed by now, but she just seemed to keep going.

"What is going on?" Ava muttered, still chasing the beam of torchlight down what seemed to be a never ending soft, pillowy tunnel.

Finally the light was getting closer and brighter. She had reached the end of the tunnel. Ava blinked at the bright white light ahead of her. The tunnel opened out into a big, soft, white land. There were fluffy trees, and little cottages that looked like they were made of pillows. It was like nowhere Ava had ever seen before. Was she dreaming?

Chapter 2

Some people rushed past Ava, not seeing her there. Well, they looked a bit like people, and yet not quite at the same time. They all looked similar, with pointed ears a bit like an elf, and soft fluffy hair that floated around them like clouds. Their eyes shone bright blue, and their skin seemed to sparkle like it was covered with a million stars. Ava couldn't tear her eyes away from them; they looked magical.

One of them must have

felt Ava staring, because she suddenly turned towards her. When she spotted Ava, her eyes opened wide in fear.

"What are you doing here?" she said.

Another two turned and they looked equally shocked.

"Who are you?" asked the second one.

"How did you get here?" asked the third.

"I... I don't know," Ava stuttered. "One minute I was in bed, looking for my torch, and then..." Ava spotted her torch on the floor just in front of her, and picked it up to show them that she was telling the truth. "Where exactly is here anyway? And who are you?"

The three huddled together, whispering quickly, then they all nodded and turned back to Ava.

"I'm Stellar, and that's Luna and Astro," said Stellar. "And we are the dream makers."

"And this is the land of dreams," said Luna.

"Where all the world's dreams are created," said Astro.

"Whoa," Ava breathed.

"No person has ever come here before," said Stellar.

"It's top secret," said Luna, and Astro nodded with wide eyes.

"I promise I won't tell anyone," Ava said, and as she looked around at the white, fluffy land around her. Even if she did tell anyone, they wouldn't believe her anyway.

"Well, since you are here…" said Stellar.

"And we've never had visitors before…" said Luna.

"Would you like us to show you around?" said Astro.

Ava couldn't find the words—she was so excited—so she just nodded.

As the dream makers led her around, Ava felt like she was walking on air. They came to a stop by a house full of dream makers in colourful lab coats, mixing up strange potions in test tubes.

"This is the imagination station," said Stellar.

"It's where all the unusual, unlikely and downright absurd dreams are made," Luna explained.

"If you can imagine it, we can make it," Astro said.

Ava watched as a scientist poured a strange liquid into

a beaker. It fizzed and spat stars. The scientist added a multicoloured fluff of cloud. Almost immediately a strange creature drifted up in a puff of smoke and swirled around the room above their heads. The scientist caught it in a pod and then sent it off along a pipe. Ava hadn't noticed the pipes before, but she saw now that there were loads of them. They snaked and looped all over the place, all leading to a huge machine in the middle of the land. Somehow Ava hadn't noticed the giant machine before, puffing and gurgling.

"What *is* that?" Ava asked, walking slowly towards it.

"That is the dream machine," Stellar told her.

"It checks all the dreams," said Luna.

"And then sends them out to the right person," Astro added.

"Whoa," Ava whispered. This place was beyond her wildest dreams.

Chapter 3

A loud alarm suddenly sounded and a red light flashed, making Ava jump.

"What was that noise?" Ava asked, spinning round.

"A bad dream," said Stellar, shaking her head.

"Sometimes dreams go bad," said Luna.

"Sometimes they go VERY bad," said Astro, looking very serious. "The dream machine catches them in the dream catcher, and they get removed."

Ava looked up to see what looked like a huge sparkling spider web above them. Lots of little floating dreams were stuck to it. They wriggled about, fighting to escape, like flies. One of the dream makers was at the top of a very long ladder, clearing away the caught dreams with what looked like a vacuum cleaner.

"So how come I still have bad dreams sometimes?" Ava asked.

"Occasionally a bad dream still makes it through," said Stellar.

"They can be sneaky," said Luna.

"Very sneaky," agreed Astro, nodding.

The dream makers explained to Ava how all dreams were made and chosen specifically for each person. They even showed her how Ava's own dreams were being created there and then, but Ava was barely listening. She was too busy taking in all the strange sights, smells and sounds. The dream machine was constantly churning out pod after pod of swirling dreams. They seemed to come in all different shapes, sizes and colours. They came in through the tubes, and then were pushed up out through the top of the dream machine up to all the sleeping people in the world above. Ava was fascinated by it all.

Then Ava noticed a big golden button on the side of the machine inside a protective plastic case.

"What does this do?" Ava asked.

"That is a very serious button," said Stellar.

"The most serious button there is," said Luna, eyes as wide as full moons.

"That is the Dream-Come-True button," Astro proclaimed. "It brings your dreams to life."

"It is only used in very special circumstances," explained Stellar.

"A Dream-Come-True button?" Ava breathed. That sounded amazing. She couldn't understand why they wouldn't use it all the time. What could be better than having your dreams come true?!

Ava wanted to ask the dream makers more about it, but when she turned around, they had already wandered off, explaining the difference between dreams and daydreams. They were so busy talking they hadn't even noticed that Ava hadn't followed them.

Ava glanced back at the button. Surely it couldn't do any harm to give it a little press, could it? She quickly pulled up the plastic case and gave the big golden button a push. She waited a moment, but nothing seemed to happen. The dream machine just gurgled and creaked the same as before, churning out dreams left, right and centre. She pressed the button a couple more times, but still nothing seemed to be happening. Maybe the button didn't work after all.

The dream makers finally noticed that Ava was no longer with them, and turned around to look for her. Ava didn't want to get into trouble, so she quickly rammed the plastic case back on and raced to catch up with them before they could see what she was doing. Ava couldn't help feeling a little disappointed. It would have been fun to have a dream come true.

Chapter 4

The dream makers continued to show Ava around, explaining the difference between dreams and daydreams, naps and snoozes. Ava began to feel very tired. She tried to hide a yawn, but the dream makers noticed.

"Time to get you back to bed," said Stellar.

"It will never do if you miss your dreams," Luna smiled.

"Off you go, off you go," Astro said, ushering her up some pillow steps towards the duvet tunnel she had come in through.

Ava was reluctant to leave; there was still so much that she wanted to ask the dream makers. But she had to admit she was very sleepy. She could barely keep her eyes open! She said goodbye to the dream makers and crawled under the duvet that was waiting there. When her head finally poked out the other side, she could see the familiar shadows of her room. She settled down in her comfy bed and was asleep before her head even hit the pillow.

The next morning, Ava's alarm woke her up. She groaned and rolled over. She was far too tired to even think about going to school.

"It's another perfect sunny Saturday, so get out there and enjoy the never-ending weekend!" the news reporter on the radio said in his chirpy voice.

Wait. Saturday? Never-ending weekend? This was a dream come true! And then Ava remembered. She pinched herself just to make sure. *Ow!* Yes, definitely not dreaming.

"The dream machine," she whispered to herself. "It was real. It worked!"

Ava bounced out of bed. This was going to be the best day ever! She pulled open the curtains. There wasn't a cloud in the sky. It was the perfect day. Then she heard the tinkling music of the ice cream van coming down the road. It pulled up right outside her house. Ice cream for breakfast? This really was a dream come true. Could this day get any better? Ava raced down the stairs and out the front door where the ice cream seller was already holding out her favourite ice cream: two scoops of strawberry ice cream with extra sprinkles.

Ava paused and checked her pockets, and her face fell. She didn't have any money.

"On the house," the man said, smiling kindly.

Ava couldn't believe her luck! She was just about to ask for extra sauce when something big and slimy landed on top of her ice cream. **SLOP!** Then another, and another fell all around. **SQUELCH! SPLAT!**

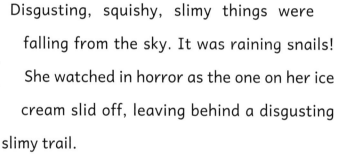

Disgusting, squishy, slimy things were falling from the sky. It was raining snails! She watched in horror as the one on her ice cream slid off, leaving behind a disgusting slimy trail.

"Ew, gross!" Ava squealed. She looked at her ruined ice cream. That was definitely not the kind of sauce she had wanted. Another snail landed with a *plop* on Ava's shoulder. With a shudder, she swiped it off and ducked for cover under a nearby tree as snails continued to rain down all around.

What was going on? Where were they all coming from?

BOOM! The ground shook vigorously. Ava stared at the floor as the snails wobbled like jelly.

BOOM! BOOM! BOOM!

The thumping got louder, and the ground shook harder with each thundering bang. The ice cream seller peered out of his van. His eyes went as wide as dinner plates, and then he sped away as fast as his van would take him. His high-pitched tinkling music played at super speed as the ice cream van zoomed down the road and away into the distance.

Ava slowly turned around, terrified of what might be there. But nothing could have prepared her for what she saw next. Stomping towards her down the street was a huge T-Rex, looming over the buildings. People were screaming, running for cover and slamming their front doors shut. Ava dropped her ice cream and turned and ran home as fast as she could. She slammed the front door shut, bolting it securely behind her.

She peered out of the window as more dinosaurs came thundering down the road. And then... was that? Surely not. A shudder ran down Ava's spine.

A huge spider—larger than a double decker bus—was crawling over the neighbour's house, wrapping all the trees and bushes in its sticky web as it went. Ava quickly pulled the curtains shut and sat on the floor. What was going on? Why were dinosaurs and giant spiders roaming the streets and snails falling from the sky? This wasn't a dream come true, this was more like a nightmare.

Then Ava realised what was happening, and it was all her fault. The Dream-Come-True button—it was making *all* dreams come true, not just the good ones but the bad ones too. She was living her worst nightmare!

Chapter 5

Ava didn't dare look out the window again. She didn't want to know what else might be going on out there. She heard her mum in the kitchen listening to the news on the radio.

"Careful if you go outside today, we are getting reports that it's raining snails out there!" the news reporter announced.

"Raining snails? Well, I've never heard that saying before," her mum chuckled to herself, shaking her head.

If only she knew, Ava thought to herself. Luckily her mum didn't have a clue about the mess that she had caused.

BANG, BANG!

The sudden hammering on the door made Ava jump. What was it now? A human-sized maggot? A man-eating toad? Ava peered out of the window and her heart sank. Even worse! It was Mr Stomp, her headmaster.

Ava ducked back down. Maybe if she stayed really quiet he would just go away.

"I wonder who that could be," Ava's mum asked, walking in.

"No, Mum, don't!" Ava hissed from her hiding place.

"Oh, Ava, there you are. I was just going to come and find you. They've just announced on the news..."

BANG! BANG! BANG!

"Alright, alright, I'm coming," tutted Ava's mum, opening the front door.

"I have come to find out why Ava didn't turn up to school this morning," sneered Mr Stomp. "And to personally make sure she gets there as soon as possible."

"But it's Saturday!" Ava said, jumping out from behind the door. Mr Stomp gave a horrible smirk.

"Didn't you hear the announcement on the morning news? I just passed a rule that means schools will now be open every day of the week. Even weekends. And anyone who doesn't attend will get a whole year's detention."

"No!" Ava cried. "This can't be true!"

"Sorry, love, but I think it is," Ava's mum said, putting her hand on Ava's shoulder. "That's what I was just coming to tell you. I'm afraid you'd better go and get your bag."

Ava stared in disbelief from Mr Stomp to her mum and back again. How could they do this to her? This couldn't be happening.

This was even worse than when it was raining snails!

The school day was worse than even Ava could have imagined. First up was triple P.E., where they had to do laps of the field in the baking sun. Ava didn't have her PE kit, so she had to wear the spare kit—it looked like it came from the Stone Age and smelled like feet. They hadn't had time to get changed afterwards, so Ava was stuck in the disgusting kit through the whole of maths. Their maths teacher was off sick, which would usually mean a fun lesson with a supply teacher—but not today. In walked Mr Stomp. He set them the hardest test Ava had ever seen in her life.

By lunchtime, Ava was dreading what kind of disgusting slop the dinner ladies would be serving up today. But then she saw the menu: jelly. Ava's favourite. At long last, things seemed to be getting better. Ava eagerly held out her dish to the dinner lady.

"Would you like an extra helping, dear?" the dinner lady asked.

"Yes, please!" Ava said excitedly, as an extra large spoonful was sloshed into her dish.

Ava took the dish hungrily but, when she looked in the bowl of delicious jelly, she noticed some big grey lumps in it.

"What's this?" Ava asked.

"Eels!" the dinner lady replied. "Jellied eels."

Ava's jaw dropped. She poked the jelly with her spoon. The eels started to wriggle—they were alive! Her stomach gave a sad, loud rumble. First she missed breakfast, and now this.

"Gross!" Ava groaned. She pushed the bowl away and picked up a piece of fruit instead. Enough was enough. She had to do something about all this mess, and fast.

Chapter 6

When it was finally home time, Ava couldn't get out of school fast enough. She rushed through the front door and did a quick check around to make sure there weren't any giant pythons or zombie sheep waiting to jump out at her. She couldn't be too careful. Then she ran straight up to her room and threw herself under her duvet. She wriggled down, on her way to the dream makers to sort out this mess, but instead she tumbled right off the end of her bed. Where were the dream makers, and why couldn't she get to them? Ava tried again, but still she found herself at the end of the bed, with no sign of the duvet tunnel or the land of dreams in sight.

"Dinner!" Ava's mum called. Ava slumped downstairs. If she couldn't get back to the dream makers, how was she going to tell them what she did and put everything right? She would be stuck in a nightmare forever!

Dinner was Ava's favourite, spaghetti with lashings of meatballs. Finally something seemed to be going Ava's way. But Ava was too miserable and too tired to enjoy it. She just pushed the meatballs around on her plate. Her mum could not have been more surprised when Ava turned down a second helping; normally she would be on a third portion by now. But when Ava was finished, all she wanted to do was go to bed. It had been an exhausting day, and she had been up half the night before in the land of the dreams. Ava groaned. Just thinking about the dream makers made her tummy feel funny.

She lay on her bed, and her eyes began to close. But she didn't want to go to sleep, not before she had worked out how to find a way back to the dream makers. She had to try again. She began to wriggle down the duvet, ready to fall off the end of the bed any second, but this time the duvet kept going again, just like the night before. Ava wriggled faster and faster until she reached a block at the end. That hadn't been there last time. Ava pushed at the soft barrier, but it didn't budge. She banged hard.

"Hello? Is anyone there? I need to talk to you!" Ava called.

She heard rustling and muttering the other side of the barrier.

"Please, I know you're there. I want to help. Let me in," Ava said.

"No!" came a voice that sounded a lot like Stellar.

"You can't come back here," said Luna.

"Not after what you did!" said Astro.

Ava's heart sank. They already knew what she had done. Of course they did, they knew everything about dreams.

"But if you know what I did to the dream machine then why haven't you stopped it? Why are all the dreams still coming true? And why have they all gone bad?"

Three little heads poked round the edge of the barrier. Ava could hear the alarm going off in the background, and saw the flashing red light.

"The button got jammed, the machine is broken," said Stellar.

"Completely frazzled," said Luna.

"It can't be fixed," said Astro. "And the effort of making them come true is breaking the machine. The dreams are getting mangled and turning bad. It's a disaster."

"It's fizzing and spluttering all over the place," said Stellar.

"It's going to explode!" squeaked Luna.

"And then there will be no dreams left!" Astro said sadly.

Ava gasped. "Can't you fix it?"

The dream makers all shook their heads.

Ava couldn't believe it. She had never meant for this to happen.

"I'm sure there must be some way to fix this, you can't give up. Please, just let me try to help," Ava said.

"You've done enough," Stellar said, and the three heads popped back behind the barrier.

Ava heard them walking away, muttering amongst themselves about what a disaster this was.

"What will become of us?" she heard Luna say with a sniff.

Ava sat with her head in her hands. What had she done?

Chapter 7

Ava sat by her window a while later, staring up at the night sky. She couldn't sleep. All she could think about was those poor dream makers and how she had ruined their lives. What would become of them if they couldn't make dreams anymore? And what would happen to the world if the nightmares didn't end? Ava wished she had never found the dream makers and pressed the button on the dream machine. Her eyes felt heavy. She longed to climb into bed and fall asleep, then perhaps she could wake up and this would all have been a strange bad dream, but that couldn't happen... could it?

It was then that Ava had a spark of an idea.

It might have been a little crazy, but sometimes the best ideas were. Ava just hoped that she wasn't too late. She quickly dived back under the covers until she reached the barrier between her and the land of dreams once again.

"I think I know how we can fix the dream machine!" she shouted, hammering against the barrier to get their attention. Eventually, she heard someone coming.

"Stop all that banging! Haven't you done enough damage already?" said a dream maker.

"Please listen to me, I've had an idea that just might work." She heard mutterings from inside.

"What should we do?"

"I don't know."

"Things can't get any worse."

Finally, she saw the barrier start to move, and three heads appeared again around the edge of the barrier.

"We're listening," said Stellar, and the other two nodded.

So Ava quickly explained her plan. After she had finished, the dream makers looked at each other.

"Will it work?" said Stellar.

"It just might!" squeaked Luna excitedly.

"It's worth a try," said Astro.

Stellar turned back to Ava. "You understand what this will mean, don't you?"

Ava nodded sadly. "I know," she said. "But it's the only way."

"Well then, we'd better get to work," said Stellar.

"Dreams to be made!" squeaked Luna excitedly.

"Not a moment to lose," said Astro.

Ava was about to leave when she turned back.

"I'm sorry for all the trouble I caused. Thank you for letting me into your world. Goodbye."

She took one last look at the dream makers, and then turned to leave. A tear trickled down her cheek as she crawled back along under her duvet and snuggled up back in bed. If everything went to plan, she would never see the dream makers again, or have any memory that they even existed.

Chapter 8

Back in the land of the dream makers, the scientists were busily putting together an exact mixture to create the perfect dream to send to Ava—the key to fixing all their problems. The dream machine creaked, shook, rumbled and huffed angrily behind them. It wasn't sounding good. They had no idea how much time they had left before it gave up completely, but they knew it couldn't be long. They just it needed to send this one last dream and make it come true.

"It's ready," the scientist finally said, passing the captured dream carefully to the dream makers. They held it delicately in their hands, watching the swirling colours.

Inside was the dream that Ava had never found her way to the land of dreams, had never met the dream makers, never pressed the golden button. If the dream machine could make this particular dream come true, then everything would be back to normal. It was possibly the most important dream they had ever created.

"Let's hope this works," said the Stellar.

"For the sake of our land," said the Luna.

"And the whole world," said the Astro.

They placed the precious dream into the tube and sent it on its way. They watched as it shot along the looping tubes towards the dream machine. The dream machine groaned and gurgled, and with one final puff, it shot the dream up into the world above, before sighing to a complete stop. This was it. Their last hope. If this didn't work, all their jobs, their whole world, everything, was finished.

Chapter 9

Ava woke to the sun streaming in through the crack in her curtains. She walked over and drew them back. It was the perfect day... then she gasped and jumped backwards. She took another peek through her curtains and laughed at herself for being so silly. A snail was sliding slowly down her window. For a crazy moment there, Ava had thought it was raining snails! She shook her head. It had felt so real for a moment, she could almost feel a snail sliding down her shoulder, and a shudder ran down her spine. Maybe it had happened in a dream.

From under her covers, unseen by Ava, three pairs of eyes peeked out at her. They smiled as they watched her.

Everything was just as it should be. The dream machine was working perfectly again, the dream makers were back to making dreams, and dinosaurs and giant spiders were no longer roaming the streets.

"Well, that's that then," whispered Stellar. "Everything is back to normal."

"The world is saved," said Luna. "We did it."

"She did it too," said the Astro. "And she'll never have any idea."

And then they all slid back under the covers and slipped away, as silent as a dream.

Discussion Points

1. How did Ava enter the land of dreams?

2. What does Ava do to make everyone's dreams come true?

a) She mixes up a potion

b) She asks the dream makers nicely

c) She presses the Dream-Come-True button

3. What was your favourite part of the story?

4. What is being served for lunch at school?

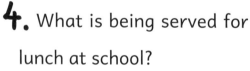

5. Why do you think the dream makers stop Ava coming back into the land of dreams?

6. Who was your favourite character and why?

7. There were moments in the story when Ava makes **mistakes**. Where do you think the story shows this most? Does she find a way to make up for her mistakes?

8. What do you think happens after the end of the story?

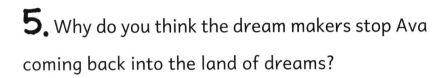

Book Bands for Guided Reading

The Institute of Education book banding system is a scale of colours that reflects the various levels of reading difficulty. The bands are assigned by taking into account the content, the language style, the layout and phonics. Word, phrase and sentence level work is also taken into consideration.

The Maverick Readers Scheme is a bright, attractive range of books covering the pink to grey bands. All of these books have been book banded for guided reading to the industry standard and edited by a leading educational consultant.

To view the whole Maverick Readers scheme, visit our website at

www.maverickearlyreaders.com

Or scan the QR code to view our scheme instantly!

Maverick Chapter Readers

(From Lime to Grey Band)

Pink
Red
Yellow
Blue
Green
Orange
Turquoise
Purple
Gold
White
Lime
Brown
Grey